When Mu Meets Min

When Mu Meets Min

Written by SHEN Shixi

Illustrated by SHEN Yuanyuan

STARFISH BAY
CHILDREN'S BOOKS

My best friend, Cheng, gave my wife Lian and I a little, white puppy named Min.

Min was a smart dog. She knew to bark if we were in danger, and she was very friendly with everyone.

My house was often full of rats, and in the middle of the night, I heard them running on the roof. They ran all over the beams and ate whatever they could find. They nibbled through bags of rice stacked against the wall and stole the cooked meat hanging from a pillar.

You wouldn't believe it, but once, two rats fought on the roof beams and fell down onto our bed. Lian was terribly frightened!

So, we decided to buy a small cat in the hope of frightening the rats away.

"Cats and dogs can't be friends," said Cheng. "They'll chase each other. They won't be able to live under the same roof."

"That's not true," I laughed.

"Dogs and cats can be friends. Cats eat fish; dogs eat bones, so they won't fight over food. The cat will chase the rats, while the dog will be in the yard guarding the house. They won't have fights because they'll have different duties."

The cat was very friendly. She had big eyes and fluffy, yellow fur. Her long tail was very soft and looked like a flag when it was standing up. Lian named her Mu.

Even though Mu was only two months old, she was already very brave. Her meow was so loud that it scared the rats away!

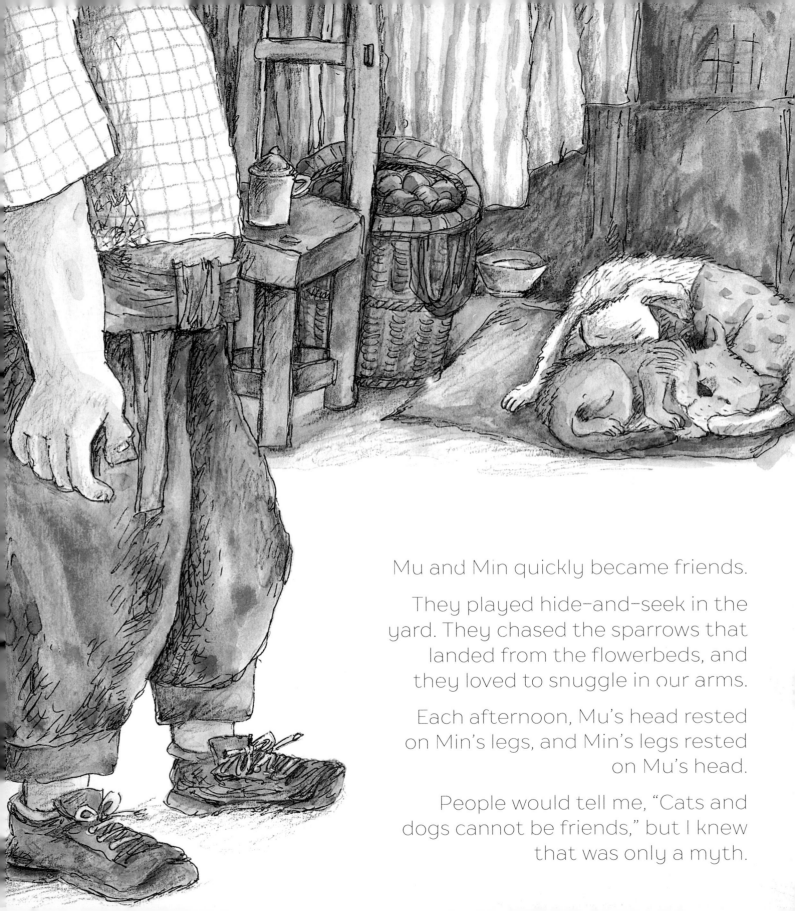

Mu and Min quickly became friends.

They played hide-and-seek in the yard. They chased the sparrows that landed from the flowerbeds, and they loved to snuggle in our arms.

Each afternoon, Mu's head rested on Min's legs, and Min's legs rested on Mu's head.

People would tell me, "Cats and dogs cannot be friends," but I knew that was only a myth.

Three months later, Mu had grown so much bigger. She jumped on the roof beams and chased the rats away. Min had grown up, too, and she always came with me to hunt in the mountains.

But over time, Min and Mu had grown apart.

One autumn afternoon, Mu was lying in the sun, making a deep, rhythmic sound: gululu, gululu...

If you've ever owned a cat, you'll know that meant Mu was feeling peaceful and happy.

But when Mu purred, Min stood up with
her tail flat, ears upright and eyes wide.
She crouched low toward Mu,
making a nasty snarl.

If you've ever owned a dog, you'll know this meant Min was getting angry. She thought Mu's purring was growling.

But Mu just kept purring and Min could no longer bear it. She barked as if to say, "I've never annoyed you. Why are you angry with me?"

Mu jumped up with fright. Her back was hunched and her tail pointed.

"What's wrong with you?" Mu growled grumpily.

We were worried they would hurt each other, so Lian and I separated them quickly.

Mu liked quiet time to herself, while Min was always friendly and excited. Mu was quite unfriendly, while Min was always outgoing.

When Min wanted our attention, Mu looked gloomy and disappointed.

I put Min down and turned to comfort Mu, but she ran silently under the bed.

Once, I went away for two weeks. When I returned, Min jumped two feet high and plunged into my arms. I felt so happy to see her too, so I hugged her tight and gently patted her.

But Mu was jealous and rushed to Min and bit her. She fled to the roof with a mouthful of white fur.

After that, the two always fought.

Whenever Mu won, Min cried like a baby. But when Min won, she barked and chased Mu around the yard. Mu chased Min's shadow. Min was ready to fight whenever she heard Mu's meow or purr.

The fights moved from inside the house to the courtyard and went from dawn until midnight. The house became a battleground for the cat and dog!

Just when we had decided to give one of them away, our poor cat had an accident. Nobody was home when Mu tried to grab a mouse so eagerly that she slipped and fell.

Splash!

Mu was stuck in the water tank. She couldn't climb up, and she couldn't jump out.

"Help! Help!" she cried.

Only Min was at home. She heard Mu's plea for help.

And whenever Min wagged her tail, showing her happiness, Mu turned away or hid.

Now, they weren't bothering each other. Now, the two could become friends again.

"This is the first time I've ever seen a dog and a cat getting along in the same house," said Cheng.

"Dogs and cats can be friends," I said, "once they learn to get along."

www.starfishbaypublishing.com

WHEN MU MEETS MIN

This edition © Starfish Bay Publishing 2017
First published in 2017
ISBN: 978-1-76036-034-4
Originally published as "Mao Gou Zhi Jian" in Chinese
© New Buds Publishing House (Tianjin) Limited Company, 2012
Printed and bound in China by Beijing Shangtang Print & Packaging Co., Ltd
11 Tengren Road, Niulanshan Town, Shunyi District, Beijing, China

Sincere thanks to Courtney Chow, Marlo Garnsworthy, Lisa Hughes, Christina
Phung, Belinda Piscino and Elyse Williams (in alphabetical order) from Starfish
Bay Children's Books for editing and/or translating this book.

Starfish Bay Children's Books would also like to thank Elyse Williams for her
creative efforts in preparing this edition for publication.